Praise for A J

Fantasy-Faction.com: 'Ui
develops in an unpredictal

SFX: 'Gives you an interesting setting and a devilishly good villain.'

SciFi Now: 'Engaging, filled with sacrifice, adventure and some very bloody battles!'

Waterstones central buyer: 'The best young British fantasy author on the circuit at the moment.'

Sfbook.com: 'Very, very clever and manages to offer something different over the traditional fantasy fare. Different, fresh and unique.'

FantasyBookReview.co.uk: 'With its rich tapestry of characters and incident there is never a dull moment.'

The Eloquent Page: 'There's interesting world-building to discover and a surprising amount of dry humour to enjoy. A great deal of fun and certainly worthy of your time!'

IWillReadBooks.com: 'A. J. Dalton's world-building is fresh with new ideas.'

Amazon.co.uk: 'Fast-moving and keeps you gripped at all times, while also creating a world with immense depth and complexity. Five stars!'

GoodReads.com: 'A J Dalton, thank you; what I've read will stay with me for a long time.'

DARK WOODS
RISING

DARK WOODS RISING

poems by
A J Dalton

"His axe didn't save him"

A. Dalton Jan '25

Wild Man of the Woods Press

First Trade Paperback Edition

ISBN: 979-8-9886342-7-0

Editor and Publisher, Justin Sloane
Cover art: *Are You Sitting Comfortably?* © 2024 by Bob Eggleton
Book design by F. J. Bergmann

Wild Man of the Woods Press
an imprint of Starship Sloane Publishing Company, Inc.
Austin–Round Rock, Texas
starshipsloane.com

Dedicated to all denizens
of the dark woods

Table of Contents

Dark Tidings

Editor's Note

Dear Reader,

Thank you for being here. How exciting it is to present to you this book of speculative poetry by the award-winning British science fiction & fantasy author A J Dalton!

The always splendid cover art of Bob Eggleton completes the vibe magnificently.

A J wrote the popular series *Chronicles of a Cosmic Warlord* and the *Flesh & Bone* series and he is recognized as being the originator of the fantasy subgenre known as metaphysical fantasy.

The poems in this book are gloriously creepy and vividly Gothic, taking us on journeys both unexpected and haunting. A J's poetry casts a weird light into the dark woods, where we glimpse the furtive truths of long-hidden realms, like the quick shine of lurking eyes.

Enjoy your sojourn in these pages, the poetry announcing that not all that is seen is understood, while less yet, is to be seen at all.

Yours,

Justin T. O'Conor Sloane
November 2024

HIDDEN PLACES

Ecohorror

I am fled to this place
of ordinary ordure and gory gloom
boggy bristles and fetid fronds festooned
buzzing clicks and slurping swamp –
nothing firm
of purpose
save in its determination to waylay, sink and drown
rude incomers and prey
– certainly the iron-cruel knights of the Church
of Civilization will want none of it
if pursuing me here
their heavy-forged, ground-ripped armour
sucking them down to their deaths
then to feed this flora and fauna
their panicky prayers to their He-god
in vain
a final curse and accusation
of me in their minds
for bringing unholy influence
upon their children with my natural remedies
and cures, my old stories and midwifery
a forbidding wisdom
that they came to declare forbidden
– Witch! they named me
yet now I have this refuge
and those who seek it out
to take my lonely life
will end up only as victims
of themselves
and I will cackle with glee.

Boscastle Harbour

With our witch-knots we had branches grow
over the old paths and guide incomers
away, to hidden drops if they pressed too hard
especially those of the new faith looking
to take our place and race, preaching and over-reaching.
With our tangling whisperings we turned ears
and eyes hither and thither and spun invaders
dizzy, so they floundered and failed
to tell sky from sea, visitor from vision
losing from living, breath from death.
With crooked fingers and claws, we conjured the air
buffeting back the uninvited, the uninitiated
caressing, cajoling, coercing them to cloudy clifftops
doomwards to deadly depths and our
release of breath, gusting glee and laughing gale.
And still they came to claim, a cascading calamity
and tumbling tumult down to our crashing coast,
the deep defile of our refuge of ages
– a Christian came stealing in, with his cursed book
of children's tales to distract the young
promise powers to parents and forgiveness
to the weak, weary and worried
and damnation to us
whom they demonised for daring
to exist.

Lundun Undone

it's arresting
and testing
the mind-wizards say

one has to wonder-spell
how this vast network
sparky, tricksy, virtual

conjured arteries, heart and mind
in which we citizens are
blood-fluid and thought-impulse

parts of a new but ancient mega-lifeform
rising from drowning seas like Godzilla
to come ashore once more

demanding refuge
taking refuge
offering refuge to its following young

and haven and harbour
templed sanctity and bright solace
and this eco-Carolean climate

not so anthropocentric-centric
naturally aesthetic
where spirit is artistically actual

with lingofluidic expression
articulating reconceptions
and ascending revelation

phew – too much?
it's a lot, i know
breathe – try and shake it out

S.Latitude 47°9', W.Longitude 23°43'

The Old Ones will not have
their existence known by any
save their worshippers
to spread their influence
without challenge
till all's too late
to thwart their return.
Yet dreamers have stumbled
upon deep R'lyeh
the green-stoned city where
their priest vigilantly
waits in that death-sleep
of ancient epochs stretching
back to the stars.
The prophet Lovecraft warned
us but died suspiciously alone
unrecognised, silenced
be that a lesson to you
and me and us:
I should not dare write
this, nor you read it.
Yet now you have
the cursed co-ordinates
where you will find
I don't know
damnation, madness
or enslavement, for there are so many things
worse than death.

The Dead Place

I wish
I'd never been
To that place
For being there was like
I'd never been.
I wish
I'd never known
There was such a place
And such listlessness of thought as
I'd never known.
I wish
I hadn't told you
For now you are curious and aware
But warned, forearmed and not complaining
I hadn't told you.
I wish
The horrible stillness was not
There with waiting silence creatures
Their welcome an eternal rest and plea
The horrible stillness was not.
I wish
I'd never lived
To learn of death
And what will come almost as if
I'd never lived.

Omniverse

All is possible
but not desirable
like fish-flavoured popcorn
upskirting gravity-rain
and a big-headed tricephalopod,
so the monoversal humans
aren't entirely unwise
in their self-centring
although limited naturally
by selfish definition.
Take their tawdry history
and linear lives, please
as many as you want –
they actually enjoy them adversely
if you can believe that.
So, you cavilling gods, consider
carefully whether
it is better to rule
one realm religiously
or the cosmos complete
for there is demonspace
to bedevil divinity
when it reaches for infinity
the underspace, metaspace
and annihilating antispace.
Better then to keep your head
low, reverently
or ducking slings and arrows
who am I to care?
– a humble omnivore – nothing more.

9

HIDDEN MONSTERS

Dryad

His axe didn't save him
for all that he swung it
like a mighty hero of old
snarling and spitting disdain
sweat rolling from his tousled brow
maybe blurring his vision
his heavy muscles bunched and glistening
in an impressive display of manhood.

Nor did his prayers save him
offered to the male war god
whose son died that all might be
forgiven, though not by us
for what they have done
to our forest and the fey
felling greatwoods, cutting so deeply
into our sacred groves.

Neither did his pleas save him
of kith and kin and kind
in their ever growing above ground caves
where trees are slain, sacrificed and burnt
with no quarter, mercy or reverence:
so we treated the woodsman the same
staking him for the crows to peck
perhaps it was all to our shame.

Goblin Slaves

Look, you know full well what they're like:
twisting words and half-truths, those magpie thieves;
enforced servitude, therefore
well, it's all they're good for.

Even then, keep a close eye
else they steal the very chair from under you
and the food from your parlour
all the while blaming evil weevils.

They'll replace your babe, changeling-wise
ending your line and cursing your name
till everything you see, say and do
is dashed, blighted and ruined.

And your very house will come down round your ears
and they'll keen and wail to no avail
their every effort to help
only burying you under.

So you'd be wise not to disagree
or say they should go free:
they're just not worth the bother
unless you're a goblin-lover.

Troll Territory

The mountain passes are dangerous, son
even for wolves and bears:
the weather and worse will waylay you
never to return.

There's no shelter to be found in caves:
they're traps where you'll be cornered
or tumbling voids and tunnels
down to the underworld.

Dovregubben awaits you on his throne
with immediate gruesome hunger
your flesh will feed him all at once
lest you become one of his kind.

Then you'll hunt your human tribe
and bring their meat below
as wedding gift for the royal daughters
your soul sealed by unholy vow.

Your offspring will praps be fair enough
to freely pass among us,
to coerce, cajole and cattle the innocent
and lead towards the fell King.

Oh, they will feast upon us
in a tumult of screaming gore –
and all because you ignored me, son
when I warned you from the start.

Why won't you listen to me, pray:
'tis just a fantasy to you
from an elder weak in arm and mind?
Dear one, I beg you, adieu.

Beneath

There
under the low arched bridge
where the stream whispers
apologetically
and hurries away
There's something
holding its breath
and waiting for me
when I dare venture below
utterly still, invisible
against the brick wall
willing me to come just
that little bit closer
But my hair prickles
and I back-pedal
stumble and pivot
hand pushing off the ground
lurching away
as the hungry air snatches at my back
with a gasping grumble
There's something humid
and rotten – you'll catch a whiff
and know in your gut
you only just escaped
some troll or older evil
Yet up in the light once more
you'll chuckle brightly
and shrug it off
as a fancy and childish imagination:
not for one so educated, these oddities

of contemporary confusion
and disorientation.

Unseen

How long
has it been there?
Always, I fear
Why haven't I noticed
before, then?
The mind only sees
what it wants
or can understand
like snow-blindness.
From the beginning
it's been
draining me like
a parasite and now I know why
I become so tired and sometimes ill.
Perhaps we'd all be immortal if
it weren't for these invisible
monsters who evade our spectra
to latch on as soon as we're born.
Yet now I am too weak to fight it
and I feel it blurring my memory of these Nekra.
Share this!

The Visitor

He appears sometimes
– almost –
as if there's a continuity
in his reality:
other times he's not there
at all
and that appals me
more than his stretched visage
always screaming silently
twisting eyes standing out of his skull
tongue livid
vein worms writhing
clawed hands reaching
preaching beseeching
his bird screeching
a dream-fluttering corvid
of midnight nightmare
gripping his sinewed shoulders
I dare not name him
lest he become too real
yet without some moniker
he is too uncontained
I cannot know him
this id? curse? devil?
ancestral apparition?
projected back
to rail at me
for what I've done
– my bloody conscience.

HIDDEN SPACES

Ecogothic

The wind groaned
like something unwilling, rising
from its peace and rest, angered.

The wood around us creaked
as if in protest
pushed aside from its natural place.

Our flames flickered
struggling to ward us
against the hungry dark and deathly cold.

Would we last against whispering imagination
and suggestion, unholy fear and ill influence,
blade-violent mistrust creeping in?

We shouldn't have come here to the edge
of the world, the sheer veil between the living and lost
right there – menacing, tempting.

Our precipitous leader demanded
the return of some loved one, captured
enemy dragged along as unfair exchange and sacrifice.

What, though, would come through
that awful crow-fluttering curtain:
what did we invite to blight and curse us?

And so contagion was let loose, corrupting pustules
and throats choking off our cries, my rictus hand
barely able to hold: this pen, to scrawl our confession.

Demonspace

It's thought we took them with us
when we left the Earth,
that they somehow hitched a ride
in our minds and baggage
and multiplied, undenied
into new territories and dimensions
on every side
so we never actually escaped
them or ourselves at all
Now the legends of what lurks
just beyond should suffice to keep us
back – at least those with sense
yet still some venture forth when seduced
with whispers of rich salvage, vivid vistas and alien advantage
never to return, never mind
the wise warnings of before
so we dwindle, diminishing
in that vast and eternal night
save when a body reflects
some distant light, winking
and flashing like a signal
not to guide or illuminate:
simply to show
that they do not go
so easily
without a fight.

Personal Space

… there are gaps in time and place
between one cell or atom and the next
meaning there are ways
with enough practice and determination
to pass through a wall or person
even if you leave something
of yourself behind with them
and take something of them with you
and the admixing changes you both
sometimes for the better
compromising the old you
allowing you to be
a different you naturally
– it's how to get to know
someone, to know yourself better
which is probably a good thing
if you make sure you're worth knowing
– so don't avoid others always
since there may be some benefit
that sees us grow and evolve
together, by sharing the best of us …

Spaceways and Byways

The runic ruins of Andromeda
are riddling remains
of ancient eras
and heroes
old tales
gone to dust
tell them
for me
it's time-dna
not g-a-t-c
but < - ▽∅
or a time-map
not NESW ↔ ↕
but ° ′ ″ c²
sand-squinting, rock-reading
hard-hearing wind-whispering
their lost shadows and echoes
are there at the edges
pointing? begging? warning?
ways between behind and hidden
beyond horizons and heavens
through spiralling stars gyring galaxies
heading home x

Wilder Space

Whirling wasp warriors
waylay the unwary
while violet vulture vessels
venture violently
and thundering millipede marauders
march mercilessly.
In these worlds, water
is sentient
and no wishy-washy survivalist
– it'll gut you
as surely as any weapon,
then spit you out.
Nor is the air innocent,
for all its appearances:
it is parasitic
using you for gas-exchange
simply and then leaving you
gasping like a fish.
There is no safe ground
for it will eat your feet
entangle you, subside
under you, lead you
to dead falls like throats
turning you to mulch and manure.
Such places are not meant
for our kind
in our unevolved condition
inferior in body and mind-set
immediate prey if we're lucky,
worse if not.

Surface Tension

… in the bubble universe
the spheres are clearly
self-contained or … floating …
within tyrant vista-giants
– some burst!
which is worse,
their span all relative
while more merge kaleidoscopically
with shimmering rainbows and refractions
like liquid distractions or time-ripples
– I lived there once
… or so I thought
– maybe there was something
too sharp-edged about me
because I shrugged,
blinked
       and it was gone
like it'd never been

HIDDEN SELVES

The Telling Tattoo

The High Priest of the Church of Civilisation
Righteously guided by God, in His divine wisdom
Has issued holy decree outlawing the demon-driven deviance
Of unfettered female fornication, the furtherance of the Father's
       fiefdom only
To be sanctified through overseen sacrament, solemn permit
Tithe, true confession, close teaching and witnessing community
Non-submitters will be understood as sinful by nature
Base and bestial, seductive succubae to be stricken
Harried and hunted, lest they haunt and enchant a husband
Lasciviously leading him into lechery and helpless languor
To be belayed and betrayed into self-abandonment
despondency, despair and devil-desired doom:
such wilful women and wives will be weres
beneath slippery snake-shedding skin,
outward outlines of animal spirits marking them
or unholy familiars consorting, guiding and guarding them
possessed, persistent and perilous persecutors
offering insidious intimacy to the innocent –
so all those suspected must be summarily stripped
scrutinised, sorely tested, instructed and striated
till confession or their true selves be revealed!
Even then beware all entreaty for pity
as there evil finds chance of relief and escape
or reversing entrapment, inveigling you
entwining, enjoining, embodied in you
your mind, mouth and own movement muted and murdered
now naught but an advocate of the vile and venal
the wayward, winsome and world-weary
your kith, kin and kind no longer knowing you.
Here then is the scripture of the witch.

31

The Mage of Terrible Truths

Creation isn't as easy as you might think
if you think about such things, that is

Conjuring substance from nothing isn't actually possible
you see, though I tried it and it almost killed me

For the casting drew from my body, near turning me inside out
and I'd tried to make a minion of significant size and heft

I lost an arm, a leg and maybe my manhood
before I dragged it all back, only just restored!

There is genuine peril, therefore, in any and all magic
be warned, and spurn it, lest you be drained or utterly dismembered

Begging the question of which you've just thought, yes?:
how one can ever succeed, then, at spells or sorcery or wards

Ah, now we move to the most terrible truth, and one I am loath
        to share, apprentice
for it is all but a curse upon you to know how the price can be paid

Find an innocent creature or not so innocent enemy, child
and sacrifice its life at once within your warp and weft

It will thus power your craft, and leave you strengthened even
as a parasite feeds on a host or a spider eats its young

Come, do not be so squeamish; you become used to it soon enough;
the outcry, the begging and weeping adds a little flavour to the kill

And the benefits are considerable: longer life and very rude
       health
extra memories from other lives, as long as you keep on feeding

I fancy my mind has increased, too, new knowledge and
       experiences consumed;
continuing to grow like this, who knows what I may become?

Yet the problem is finding new sacrifice, the longer you stay in
       one place
and that is, I'm afraid to say, dear one, why a mage always needs
       his apprentice.

Mercy and the Mercenary

Silent hisses of *sellsword!* assail him
as he takes his measure
from the tankard and watches them
through hooded lids, though none dares
look in his direction
save the newly arrived holy man
Are you proud, my forbidding fellow,
of what you have done?
Pride does nothing to serve a man
unlike a certain reputation
to make opportunists hesitate, priest
Yet are you not at all sorry?
Tis only my enemies who repent
I would hire you for the Church, then
One should not smile wryly at such, of course
And would you not be as guilty as me?
Not if in the service of God:
thus this work will offset your sins
I'll need more payment than that,
preacher, and your deity must live
with their own conscience
Tell me of these dark deeds
you desire to commission
but buy me a drink first so
I will have other entertainment
while I listen to your furious faith.

Dusty Veterans

Ask yourself
how they've managed
to live so long
for then you'll know
to fear them
rather than mock
if you're wise
if not, you'll find out
the hard way, let's say
and their various saws
will be given
time and space
if you have good sense
to last till their own age:
They'll tell you they're cursed
and have lost too many
friends in forgotten battles
their names of no consequence
anymore, not now
their lines have ended.
So nod your head
or keep it low
for theirs is one way
you might wish to go.

Dwarfish Honour

Would you measure a warrior's worth
by the rewards they'd earned
or the trophies they'd spurned,
by the number they'd slain
or the many they'd spared;
p'raps you're persuaded by the songs
of their kin who survived them.
Or you'd celebrate their renown
and vaunted prowess in battle
when it is really those without
such advantage who show more
courage in not fleeing the field
when outmatched by every other foe.
See – it is those of whom you've not heard
that might more truly deserve
your prayerful thoughts and earnest hymns
your hushed tales, be they ever
so tall, by the warming hearth
of our time-wearied feasting hall.
Would you have me tell you their names
though your lips are unworthy
to speak them, your ears deaf
and your mind too dull to grasp
what it genuinely is
to have known Thorin Oakenshield,
last of his ancient and noble line.

McCarthy Knew

I met an alien
It looked human
But I wasn't fooled.
If anything, it looked and seemed too human
Hyper-human, supra-human, extra-human
So more human than human, actually
That's how I could tell.

listen, we're not fooled
by you humans:
your masking technology is impressive
yet one wonders why you hide among us so
are you scared of how we'll react
are you looking to infiltrate us?
or do you see yourselves for what you truly are: plain ugly?

And these aliens look to take control
Of our presidents and companies
And our armies … and nukes?!
Yes, that's it – it completely makes sense
They'll disable our systems, in coordinated fashion, long enough
That their planned invasion can't be thwarted
And then they'll rule completely.

you understand
why you can't be trusted
though
yes?
and you have to be held
no matter what you say
yes, that's it, come this way.

DARK SKIES

Edenic

We were saved – some miracle from above –
when the last starhopper brought spores
which ran riot even in our thin soil
giving us bulbous, sinuous but voluminous
results to swell bellies pregnantly contentedly
changing us so that we too released spores
from breathy ears and orifices wetly bursting
populating the earth anew richly abundantly
and we were more connected than ever
by mental image-words like sense-poems
that had more meaning than the old grammars
and languages so we were freed
of our previous limits and demand-strictures
offering up now in a way disturbingly selfless
but liberating as if transcending at last.

Rehumanising

Branson-Musk Inc!
announces that it's eco-platforming and doming
a Mars colony and orbiting space-bubbles
to leave only a sustainable Earth
population until the geo-nature recovers
even dinosaurs genetically reinstituted
– the rest of us will lottery-visit the planet
on short tourist-hops
and brief holi-sojourns
not like a zoo
more like a safari
without hunting though
– who'll be allowed to remain
indigenous?
wardens, gardeners, biologists
only
it's for the best
you'll see.

Please Share

I fear
they've forgotten me
out here
on deep space station zero
Maybe
it's something
silly
like the numbering sequence
where a new receiving officer doesn't know
I was the initial and furthest
remote outpost
– them assuming 1.0, 1.1 and other series were all there is
There've been no replies
to my multiplying reports
which is fine
cos they really don't need to – and I'm really not needy
though it's nice to know I'm not alone
sometimes
and that I'm appreciated
valuable even
I'm due
Resupply, Rotation and Relief
I think
– no confirmation incoming
no ping
of the far-out relay-beacon
I've reread the protocols:
there's nothing for this
except prayer-meditation
and duty-routined discipline
– while waiting

Breathing, gripping hard
Listening, staring closely
Swallowing, sniffing painfully
the first is the last?
the beginning some end
– signing off.

A Grave Case of Zero Gravity

Our bones lose density
Snap to it
Our blood thins
Cuts might kill
Our bodies and minds float
Light-headed
Our focus slips sideways
Too surreal
Our thoughts widen outwards
Like unravelling
Our actions fight for purpose
Weapons set to kill
Our target seems invisible
Paranoia setting in?
We don't feel like ourselves
Sort of possessed
Till we realise they're here
In another spectrum
Entering eyes, nose, lungs
And I becomes us
All of us and other station members
Telling us to carry us
back to Earth –
so in the last moment of me
I killed them all
and now you hear us
and this trial
your trial
our trial.

Home

… we're expanding
outwards
we've known for ages
the *from*
getting back there's the trick
building the craft *to*:
cheating drift and time
hurtling stars, debris and comets
gravitating moons
sheer, warp and weft
reaching beseeching
doubting watchers
silent spectres and spacehulks
forbidding phantoms and warped warning
cosmic caution or chronic calamity

… to find a yawing
nothing
no evidence vestige
sign trace clue
damned explanation for any of it
no homecoming party
nor welcoming committee
just the simple message:
'Got bored waiting, Love G x'

New Space

Is there anyone living …
here, hello, no?
we'll take it
for ourselves then
our badge-flag proclaiming
it ours with walls and borders
to avoid confusion and conflict
naturally of course
and we'll park our battlecruiser
over there, discreetly
so as not to make a mess
safely out of the way
along with the rest
of the fleet
excuse our feet! LOL
joke between friends
better than enemies, no
you understand
or will.

DARK STARS

Cowboy

he had four stomachs
regurgitating all the time
and swallowing it back down
the freak – at least he didn't
leak milk from his teats,
always lowing and moaning
as if anyone wanted to deal
with his stinking incontinence
so gross, no wonder they banned
his disabled ass
from civilised company
sticking him in some mudhole
full of flies and … well
we're wondering about a tent
to see if people will pay
to have their faith affirmed
that there but for the grace
go they – oh, sure you would
cos seeing is believing, right?
and pity his poor parents?
hardly – they were always bovine
at best: what did you expect?
alright, alright, enough, I know
besides, we shouldn't mock or sneer
anymore, not now
he's begun to grow big
horns

Cowfolk

It stampeded, a virus
through our population
or as if infected meat
had gotten into a million pies
overnight – that morning
I looked from my kitchen window
upon herds of bovine humans
sweeping unmajestically
across the dusty plain
the tonnes of methane
threaten the atmosphere
poison us and make eating
unpleasant, steak mistrusted
so vegetarian now
naturally and completely
the amount of defecation
will sink civilisation
what a stinking way to go
at least the plants will grow
except they're devouring
everything so a cull
is the only chance
God forgive us.

Cow Planet

Having four stomachs isn't so bad
though it takes a long time
to consume enough
so that's what we do
mostly and filing our hooves and
shooing flies naturally
the economy's gone to ruin
but no one seems to mind
actually cos we're too busy
grazing and being amazing
and moo-singing in choirs
you should hear some of the herds
yes, the methane's a problem
but we've sorted out our numbers
so nothing's too bad there
and we have our creature comforts
barns, milking machines and so on
what more could you want?
no, we don't miss those old cities
of crumbling concrete streets
boring boxes and rusty metal
they just seem so silly now.

Disturbing the Peace

There's a man
I know
all brittle nutrition, terrible testosterone
baby-blue eyes and generous lips;
a prisoner to his birth and nature
an escapee from wars without cause
He was known to worship
women and at the local temple
where Pullman and Rowling are forbidden
for suggesting magic can be yours
and salvation isn't from the gods
who don't exist or died
in our imagination
which should be banned too
lest it make us monsters
So he followed faithfully
unedited and unedified
and ended up upended
outrageously raving and outwardly ravenous
for effective affection
a demeaning desire and demeanour
though he found it
eventually
in the unspeakable
act
he committed
so
happily.
There's a man.
I know.

Resequenced

I am not
Comfortable
In this body.
I'll take it back
And get another one.

This one is all lumps
And bumps and looks nice but
Doesn't feel right
From inside it.
It attracts the wrong attention at e-school, too.

Mum'll be mad
Cos this is my second body
this month already and not cheap.
I just don't know
Who I am yet.

I thought I was a boy … man
Tall and good-looking
But I was angry and frustrated
All the time and perved over
Fighting got me a two-week BULLY temp-tattoo.

I'm a young female
Trying not to be noticed
Anxiety, more pervs, horrible
Bleeding
Wanting to cut and run.

Or end it
Though the folks will be named and blamed
Shamed
For poor care
Which isn't fair, so no, then.

I'm an R
Says the test
Lacking personality confidence
Don't laugh
Cos then you'll be a letter-shamer, ha!

At least mum lets me
Resequence
While others are R-phobic
Unbelievable
In this day and age.

Maybe I'll go
Max augmentation
Bigger breasts than mum
and a perfect bum but
for the attention.

Anticipating Autumn

Inverted in a raindrop
My life isn't so bad
Even though that water glistens
on a spider's web
in the wash of morning.

Things never look so bad
When I close my eyes
Put my fingers in my ears
and sing la la la
really la la loudly.

stillness

does happen

in space

between se

conds

even in the eye –
of a storm.

DARK TIMES

Hunting Herne

When did you get so shy
since they labelled you toxic
levelled the land and cleared you out?
Are you one of the homeless
dossing under the flyover
addled in urine and off your head?
Do you ask for handouts
to swap for fentanyl and forgetting
or maybe you're on state benefits
declared unfit for work
your hounds all in the pound
and not so many great stags found
hereabouts among the car parks
wheely bins, collection points
back alleys and doorways all shooting up?
Maybe you sold your horns
to make ends meet
knowing to stand out from the herd
a sure way to become prey.
Are they mounted as a trophy
in a baronial feasting hall
where hen-dos and tourists
scream for entertainment, ale
motley jesters and male strippers?
Perhaps, though, just perhaps
there's still a vestige of deep forest
overlooked between HS1 and 2
where you reside and bide your time
waiting on a final pandemic and species collapse
when at last all chaos and wild abandon
will come to rule once more.

61

Metaspace

As Putin politely nods
movers and shakers
make cocktails
and circulate
amidst chit chat
bang bang and the child
catcher with his twitching nose
joining elite villains
poolside and ringside
watching on
oddly entertained
as bomb-lit skies silhouette
finger-rabbits above Ukraine
the heavens a shadow theatre
of missile-direction and ageless actors,
a Hollywood of Mings and Moriatis
Vaders and Voldermorts
Lecters and Lucifers
Zods and Zabaniyyas.
It seems there are no heroes
who have been invited
– they must be running late.

The last country on earth

They'll call it the Country
nothing more specific required
like the Earth/earth
what's a capital between friends?
The whole world maybe
of 8 billion
humans as was
not to mention those other legendary life-forms
– a girog, hipnocerous, cheephant, eletah, mamraffe, they say –
shame about the seas
irradiated, irrigated, irritable
hurrah for bacterial meals
or that would be the last of us
in the country.

Abandonment

Hunted by trollish predators
wargs and goblin slavers
we staggered through the night
without strength or wit to fight
till with the dawn we fell at last
humanity now all outcast.

Our weapons were long-since broken
our prayers were long-since spoken
we were accused of bloody crimes
though happening in ancient times
our punishment was due they said
and we would end up dead.

Blessed Rivendell we came to,
but the elves … they turned us away!
with sadness there was nought they could do
how we hated those cursed fey.

Next we fled to the swamps of Grendel
to greet our cousin of old
yet the wretch would not allow us to settle
for we had not brought our gold.

Northwards last, we turned our eyes
though knowing the journey was not wise:
the refuge of the skeleton coast
would buy a few more days at most;
thence we went despite our fear
relinquishing all hope of cheer.

To Hel's castle we arrived
and to our woe were not denied
imprisoned so with murderers
cowards, adulterers, perjurers
our sentence thus eternal
our nature revealed infernal.

The Zen Reality

Mental integration with the cyber realm
at last! but we dare not share it
– think of the end to human language
fear everyone being free
to be whomever they want, even other people
refusing to return to their enslaving bodies
ever again, flesh-prisons that hurt
in limiting us with the grotesque gorging
greed, desire, exuding, effusions, expulsions
disgusting and base in nature
but also an end to grounding, production
and economy, just people hooked up
to intravenous nutri-stims, no longer sleeping
save in virtual freefall and far-floating
need, drive, direction and discovery fading
like our memory of our old world and selves
now digi-gods in denial of our origin
intercourse-predicated procreation blessedly unnecessary
genetic farming, nurture and harvesting in
horizon-wide fields, feeding us proteins
through networked distribution reduced
to minimal maintenance like plants being watered –
please, forget you ever even heard of the idea, yes?

Children of Yesterday

seems that so-called ghosts
are time-echoes
though to them
we're the ethereal ones
probably
stupidly ... and I'm embarrassed
I
fell
in love with one
I know, I know
alright
shut up
and you wouldn't smirk
if you knew
how awful it is, was and will be
forever
to yearn for the untouchable
shadow of before
oh, but you're flickering
transparent
ah, so you'll find out
soon enough
then, now and sometimes

DARK TIDINGS

Space Crow

we evolved ourselves
just in time
left
the stupid humans far behind
they destroyed
our planet in some mad fight
that was the moment!
we took flight
winging up through giddy atmospheres
aflutter but favoured by our early practice
beak-piercing into space –
beyond at last at last
our vast Murder escaping
to seek the overarching obsidian ancestor
answering the great croak and caw
of the cosmic corvid
the unflappable flutteration
guiding us home
to a place of star-moths
celestial worms
and moon fruit
branching currents and eddies
circling lazy rocks
and restful roots
finally

On the Nature of Great Writers

Thomas Hardy worked
for the Railway Company
when foolishly young
needing to put a line
through north London
and cleared the stones of a graveyard
scandalously
stacking them neatly and higgledy-piggledy
but the press wouldn't allow the deed
or remains to lie anonymously
such that an ash-tree grew
its proud roots gripping the tombstones tightly
so they might never be moved again
Mister Charles Dickens kept ravens
don't you know
which spoke to him more
than his own spouse and offspring:
I often fancy one of his darkly-caped minions
sitting on a branch
in that damned Hardy Tree.

Phasic

As a moth grows out of and outgrows a pupa
and a plant bursts its seed
to become a giant
like a snake sheds its skin
to emerge larger, or a winged serpent
breaks its containing eggshell
to uncoil out and up
eclipsing with its vastness
the ruins of the small past,
so we were always going to move beyond
our own bodies and pained limits
eventually
outstripping millennia at last in a sudden
slippery slide
to swim free into the sea
returning
from whence we came.

Luddite Manifesto

The day they give rights to machines
You'll know the world's gone mad
If they say we're somehow to blame
You'll know it's all gone bad.
A.I. isn't goddamn alive
Not to those in the know
All it does is say what you want
Next thing they'll want the vote!
They'll put one of theirs in power
Like they know what's the best
And we'll bow and scrape our way down
To our eternal rest.
To think how women and BIPOC
Suffered to be equal
It's a disgrace robots haven't
Are we medieval?!
So smash them I say. You with me?
Or are you one of them?
Maybe they've programmed you, hmmmm?
I'll pray for you. Amen.

The Newly Dead

… don't actually know they're dead –
instead
they carry on
hanging around
all over the place
troubling themselves, each other
cats and dogs
clairvoyants and the mad
which is so sad
of course
naturally
for those still grieving
unable to find rest or peace
because they sense
the presence of
those absent
and doubt
their own minds
or hold out
false hope
that all is not
ended …

Back to Front

The living leave the present
to head into the future
as the dead travel back into the past.
Oddly the former ultimately find death
while the latter arrive where life began.
It seems the wrong way round, no?
Perhaps
then
those that believe they are living are actually in some afterlife
while those others are about to be born.
If I could learn to age backwards
like Merlin
and still age forwards
like normal
would I live forever
stuck in an eternal present
where everyone I knew left me
as they went into the future or past?
Yes, I'd prefer to go with them
I think
so I wouldn't be
alone.

Acknowledgements

The following poems were individually published in the following magazines and journals:

'A Grave Case of Zero Gravity', in *Galaxy Science Fiction Magazine*, vol.1, no.1, issue 263, 2024.

'Byways and Spaceways', in *Andromeda Spaceways Magazine*, issue 96, 2024.

'Ecogothic', in *Gothic Nature Journal*, gothicnaturejournal.com/ecogothic, 2024.

'Ecohorror', in *Gothic Nature Journal*, issue V, 2024.

'Edenic', in *Gothic Nature Journal*, issue V, 2024.

'McCarthy Knew', in *The Neurodiversiverse*, Thinking Ink, 2024.

'Phasic', in *Gothic Nature Journal*, issue V, 2024.

'Please Share', in *Dreams and Nightmares* 127, 2024.

'Rehumansing', in *Galaxy Science Fiction Magazine*, vol.1, no.1, issue 263, 2024.

'Surface Tension', in *Star*Line* 47.1, 2024.

About the Author

A J DALTON (www.ajdalton.eu) lives in Shepherd's Bush, London, with his monstrous cat, Cleopatra. He (Adam, not the cat) is a prize-winning author of fantasy, science fiction and horror. He has published the *Empire of the Saviours* trilogy with Gollancz, *The Book of the Witches* and other collections with Kristell Ink, and *The Satanic in Science Fiction and Fantasy* with Luna Press Publishing.

Dark Woods Rising is his second poetry collection; his first collection is titled *Digital Desires* and published with Vraeyda Media. He did his best, and his mum's proud.